—THE—
REWILDING
REVOLUTION

Copyright © 2025 by Prentice Batts

All rights reserved. In accordance with the U.S. Copyright Act of 1976, the scanning, uploading, and electronic sharing of any part of this book without permission of the publisher constitute unlawful piracy and theft of the author's intellectual property.

Thank you for your support of the author's rights.

The publisher is not responsible for websites, or social media pages (or their content) related to this publication, that are not owned by the publisher.

Paperback ISBN:

Publisher Disclaimer:

The publisher of this story hereby declares that it is not responsible for the content, views, opinions, or any other material expressed within the story. The story's content solely belongs to the author, and any claims, statements, or information provided within the narrative are the author's sole responsibility. The publisher does not endorse or guarantee the accuracy, validity, or completeness of the story's content, and disclaims any liability for any harm, loss, or inconvenience caused by the story's content or its interpretation.

Published in United States of America 10 9 8 7 6 5 4 3 2 1

VMH™Publishing

THE
REWILDING REVOLUTION

WRITTEN BY
PRENTICE BATTS

The Rewilding Revolution" begins with a young visionary, Ethan Rivers, who dares to imagine a world where humanity returns to its natural roots. As his dream ignites a global movement, society must confront its reliance on technology, greed, and control, questioning whether true freedom and harmony with nature are within reach. A bold journey into a future where humans and the Earth thrive together awaits.

CONTENTS

CHAPTER 1: The Spark of a Dream 1

CHAPTER 2: The First Steps 5

CHAPTER 3: Resistance and Growth 9

CHAPTER 4: A World United 13

CHAPTER 5: The Great Transition 17

CHAPTER 6: A New World 21

EPILOGUE: The Rewilded Earth 25

CHAPTER 1

THE SPARK OF A DREAM

Twelve-year-old Ethan Rivers lived in a city of glass and steel, where every inch of land was paved, and the sky was obscured by skyscrapers. Life felt suffocating. Schools taught obedience to routines, offices consumed his parents' lives, and even play was confined to tiny, artificial parks surrounded by fences. Ethan often felt like a caged bird.

One day, during a rare visit to the countryside, Ethan wandered into the woods while his family picnicked nearby. The air felt alive, the scent of pine and soil intoxicating. He removed his shoes to feel the earth beneath his feet, and for the first time, he felt truly free.

As he explored deeper into the forest, Ethan stumbled upon an ancient oak tree with carvings on its bark. They seemed to form a story of humans living harmoniously with nature—free,

Chapter 1

unburdened by possessions or clothing, and thriving under the open sky.

The carvings ignited something in Ethan's heart. He realized how far humanity had strayed from its roots. That night, he promised himself that he would change the world, bringing people back to a life of freedom and connection with nature.

CHAPTER 2

THE FIRST STEPS

Back in the city, Ethan couldn't stop thinking about the forest. He began researching ancient cultures and tribal communities that lived in harmony with the land. He learned about the Hadza of Tanzania, the Amazonian tribes, and the nomadic peoples of Mongolia. These communities needed little from the modern world and lived rich, fulfilling lives.

Ethan's passion didn't go unnoticed. His best friend, Maya, grew curious. "Why are you so obsessed with this nature stuff?" she asked.

"Because we've lost something important," Ethan said. "We're trapped in a system that doesn't make sense. Imagine if we didn't have to work just to survive or wear clothes to fit in. Imagine if we were free to live like the animals—connected to nature, without shame or fear."

Maya hesitated, then nodded. "It sounds crazy, but... maybe you're right."

Together, they began small. Ethan and Maya started a community garden in an abandoned lot, encouraging neighbors to grow food instead of buying it. They held meetings to talk about sustainability and the joy of reconnecting with nature. Slowly, more kids joined their cause, curious about this dream of freedom.

CHAPTER 3

RESISTANCE AND GROWTH

Ethan's ideas weren't popular with everyone. His parents were horrified when they found him reading about nudist movements and sustainable living.

"You're embarrassing yourself!" his father shouted. "People don't live like that anymore. You need to focus on school and getting a good job."

"But why?" Ethan asked. "Why should I spend my life working for things I don't need? There's so much more to life!"

At school, teachers dismissed him as a dreamer, and bullies mocked his idealism. Yet, Ethan's resolve only grew stronger.

He and Maya began organizing excursions into the nearby woods, where they taught their friends how to forage for food, build shelters, and navigate using the stars. They encouraged everyone to shed their shoes, and over time, some grew bold enough to shed their clothes, experiencing the liberating feeling of being one with nature.

What began as a small group soon became a movement. Kids from neighboring schools joined in, and word spread through social media. They called themselves "The Rewilders."

CHAPTER 4

A WORLD UNITED

By the time Ethan turned fifteen, The Rewilders had become a global phenomenon. They held rallies advocating for the rewilding of urban spaces and the decriminalization of public nudity. They argued that clothing was a tool of oppression, fostering shame and materialism, and that humanity's future lay in embracing its natural state.

Ethan, now a charismatic speaker, addressed crowds with passion. "We're born free, yet we spend our lives confined by walls and rules that make no sense. Let's return to the earth, to the freedom that's our birthright. Let's tear down these cities and grow forests in their place!"

Governments and corporations pushed back hard, labeling the movement a threat to civilization. But as climate disasters worsened and people

Chapter 4

grew disillusioned with modern life, more began to listen.

The Rewilders gained allies among scientists, environmentalists, and even celebrities. Ethan met indigenous leaders who shared their wisdom and joined forces with climate activists fighting for the same vision.

CHAPTER 5

THE GREAT TRANSITION

The tipping point came when a global economic collapse left millions unemployed and disillusioned with the system. Ethan and the Rewilders seized the moment, launching a worldwide campaign called "The Great Transition."

Cities became hubs of rewilding efforts. Abandoned skyscrapers were dismantled, their materials repurposed to build eco-villages. Asphalt roads were ripped up, replaced with thriving gardens. Rivers were restored, forests replanted, and animals returned to their natural habitats.

Ethan led by example, living in a communal village where no one owned possessions, wore clothes, or used money. Every need was met through cooperation and connection with the land.

At first, the changes were met with

resistance. But as people experienced the joy of living freely, without the constraints of modern society, the movement spread like wildfire.

CHAPTER 6

A New World

By the time Ethan turned twenty-five, the world had transformed. Borders disappeared as nations united under the principles of rewilding. Cities were now thriving ecosystems, where humans lived as part of nature rather than apart from it.

Clothing became optional everywhere, and shame around the human body vanished. People worked only to meet their basic needs, spending the rest of their time exploring, creating, and connecting.

Ethan, now regarded as a global leader, refused to be treated as a figurehead. "I'm not a hero," he said. "I'm just someone who listened to the earth. This world belongs to all of us."

EPILOGUE

THE REWILDED EARTH

Decades later, Ethan sat beneath the ancient oak tree where his journey began. Around him, children laughed and played, their feet bare on the soft grass. The air was filled with birdsong, and the sky was a brilliant blue, unclouded by smog.

Ethan smiled, knowing that humanity had found its way back to its roots. The dream he had as a boy—a world where everyone lived freely, connected to nature—had become reality.

And for the first time in history, the earth itself seemed to breathe a sigh of relief.

www.ingramcontent.com/pod-product-compliance
Lightning Source LLC
LaVergne TN
LVHW052049070526
838201LV00086B/5160